For information address Marvel Press,
125 West End Avenue, New York, New York 10023.

Printed in China
First Hardcover Edition, July 2015 10 9 8 7 6 5 4 3 2 1
ISBN 978-1-4847-4768-1
T425-2382-5-15194

These Are the
Guardians of the Galaxy

BOOK SIX

Los Angeles • New York

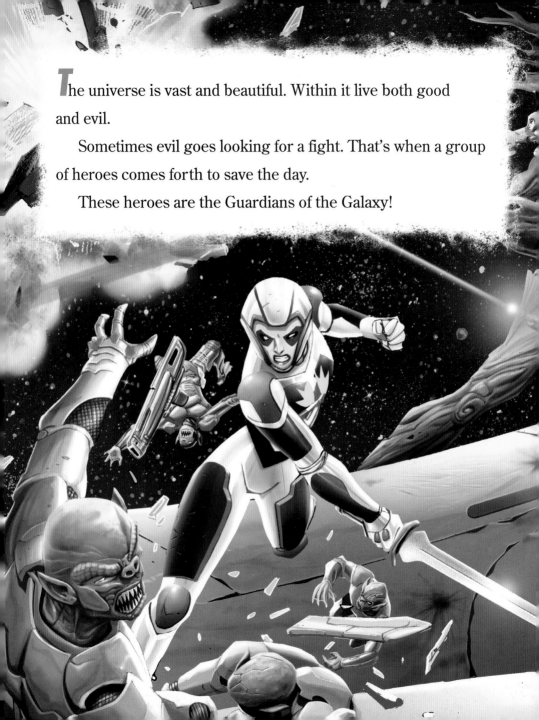

The universe is vast and beautiful. Within it live both good and evil.

Sometimes evil goes looking for a fight. That's when a group of heroes comes forth to save the day.

These heroes are the Guardians of the Galaxy!

Led by Star-Lord, the Guardians of the Galaxy vow to help those in need. But Star-Lord wasn't always a hero. Once he was just a little boy named Peter Quill.

Peter's mother knew he was special. When he was old enough, she gave Peter a box of his father's things. Peter learned that his father was from outer space, from a world called Spartax.

At night, Peter watched the stars, thinking about his father.

As Peter got older, he decided to go find his father. But to do so, he would have to reach for the stars.

Peter studied very hard in school, learning as much as he could about planets, moons, and galaxies! Eventually, Peter became an astronaut. He was ready to find his father!

Using his star maps, Peter visited several planets in search of his father. But no one had answers.

At last, Peter's ship, pushed to its limits and in need of repairs, landed on a strange world called Knowhere.

As Peter roamed the planet, he learned that a great intergalactic king had arrived. It was his father!

Peter's father was thrilled to see his son. He explained that he couldn't go to Earth because of a ruling that made the planet off-limits to all galactic empires.

Peter's father told him about a warlike empire called the Badoon. Enemy of Spartax, it would stop at nothing to destroy all good things, including Earth.

Peter knew he had to protect his home planet. His father gave him a new ship called the *Milano*. He also gave Peter special armor that empowered him. Now Peter could run faster, become stronger, and even fly!

Peter had become Star-Lord! But to protect his planet, he would need a team. . . .

First Star-Lord met Gamora.

When Gamora was very young, the Badoon enslaved her
planet. Gamora fled and was taken in by Thanos, the most feared
villain in the universe. Under Thanos's watch, Gamora became
a dangerous warrior. But after many years, she realized that
Thanos was just like the Badoon. She fled again, vowing to fight
evil, and joined Star-Lord.

Gamora told Star-Lord of a great warrior named Drax the Destroyer. Legend had it that Drax became so enraged when he lost his family to the Badoon that he defeated one of their fighter ships all by himself!

Since that time, Drax had traveled the galaxy, fighting for good.

Drax knew what it was like to lose a family, and he did not wish for anyone else to experience the pain he had felt. And so he agreed to join Star-Lord and Gamora.

Star-Lord's next stop was
Planet X: a beautiful world
filled with sprawling forests
and treelike beings who
had the ability to become
large or regrow from a
single leaf.

One particular being
took a liking to Star-Lord.
His name was Groot. He spoke
very little, only ever saying
"I am Groot," but it was clear
that he had decided to join
Star-Lord's team.

Star-Lord's last stop was the planet Halfworld. He was looking for Rocket Raccoon.

Rocket was no ordinary raccoon. He was a fierce fighter who had been given advanced skills by a group of scientists. Rocket had learned to use his talents to do what he loved best: make new weapons! And firing them at bad guys was his specialty!

So Rocket joined Star-Lord and his team.

Word traveled fast in space, and it didn't take long for the
Badoon to learn about Star-Lord's team.

A fleet of Badoon ships entered the Milky Way and headed for Earth. It was time for Star-Lord to act.

The team suited up. The Guardians of the Galaxy had been born!

The Badoon were ready to conquer Earth at any cost. But the
Guardians were ready, too. They fought with heart, battling long
and hard.

Gamora, Drax, and Star-Lord worked as a team and tore
through the Badoon with ease.

Groot grew and grew, towering over the Badoon, while Rocket used his weapons to blast the invading aliens.

When one Guardian needed help, another stepped up to lend a hand.

Finally, they defeated the Badoon.

Peter knew stopping the Badoon was a symbol of hope—for the galaxy, for Earth, and for his family and friends. He dreamed of a day when the galaxy would be a peaceful place, free from evil.

Gamora, Drax, Rocket, and Groot shared Peter's dream.

Together, the Guardians of the Galaxy vowed to make that dream come true.